THE CALL OF THE WILD

By *JACK LONDON*

Adapted and abridged by *OLIVE PRICE*

Illustrated by *DOUGLAS ALLEN*

ISBN: 0-448-02249-4 (Trade Edition)

1973 PRINTING

GROSSET & DUNLAP · Publishers · NEW YORK

A Thief In The Night

BUCK was the proudest dog on Judge Miller's big estate. He was the son of Elmo, a huge St. Bernard. All his life Elmo had been the Judge's close companion. Buck's mother was a shepherd dog from the heather hills of Scotland.

He was not as large as his father, but he weighed one hundred and forty pounds. His fur was brown and glistened with glints of red and gold. His eyes were brown, too. When he was happy they sparkled, but when he was angry they darkened and shone with such fury that neither man nor beast could tackle him.

But Buck was seldom angry in this lovely place. Judge Miller's house stood in the sun-kissed Santa Clara Valley, a beauty spot in California. It was big and spacious and approached by winding driveways. Trees and gardens surrounded it. There were great stables where a dozen grooms took care of fine horses. There were also vine-covered cottages that housed the many servants who took care of the Judge's family.

Buck loved every member of the Miller family. He carried the Judge's grandsons on his back. Sometimes he rolled them over and over merrily in the grass. And always he guarded them when they went adventuring to the paddock or the berry patch beyond.

"Buck! Buck! Buck!" He would always answer their call when they wanted a gay companion.

He took Alice and Mollie, the Judge's daughters, on early morning rambles and long twilight walks. And he went swimming with the Judge's sons. One of them would throw a ball into the pool.

"Here, Buck," he would cry. "Swim out and catch it in sixty seconds!"

And always Buck would plunge into the water and bring the ball back on time. Other dogs that lived on the estate would stand and watch him enviously.

Buck looked down his nose at them. He was four years old and king of all the dogs that lived in the kennels. There was Toots, the Japanese pug, and Ysabel, the Mexican hairless, and a whole score of fox terriers. Unlike these dogs, however, Buck was neither a house dog nor a kennel dog. He was the proud and privileged one who could go when and where he pleased. Indoors and out — yes, Buck was king!

Best of all, on winter nights he was companion to the Judge. The Judge would sit in his big chair in front of a roaring fire in the library. While he read the news, he would often talk to Buck, lying at his feet.

And so it was one autumn night in the fateful year of 1897. Buck had been hunting that day with the Judge's sons in woods that were scarlet

and gold. He was drowsy now and almost asleep when the Judge rattled his paper.

"Well, Buck," the Judge said, "they've found gold in the Klondike, up in the frozen North! Perhaps," he went on teasingly, "we should stop hunting rabbits and go look for a gold mine."

"Woof!" Buck answered, not too enthusiastically.

Judge Miller chuckled and leaned forward to stroke Buck's head.

"Gold in the Klondike," he repeated. "It will be like a call to men in all parts of the world. Thousands of them will risk their lives in that arctic darkness to find the fortunes of their dreams."

"Woof!" Buck snickered again, only to please the Judge, of course. He could not know what this rush for gold would ever mean to him . . .

But even now, the gold rush was casting its shadow on Judge Miller's house. He had spoken of the men who would go to the Klondike. He had not really thought of the dogs they would need.

And neither Buck nor the Judge could know that there was one on the estate who had heard of the gold rush too. One who had thought of the dogs that would go even more than the men. Yes, the gold rush meant real trouble for every tidewater dog with warm long hair and good strong muscles, from Puget Sound to San Diego.

It was Manuel, the gardener, who was the treacherous one. He knew that dogs were needed to pull men's sleds in the Klondike, and Manuel needed money. Never was there enough to pay for his gambling debts. And, of course, Buck couldn't remember — but Manuel had looked at him that very afternoon and had said to himself:

"You, Buck! You are strong and would make a good sled dog! Why shouldn't you pay my debts?"

The following night Judge Miller went to a meeting of the Raisin Growers' Association. His boys were busy with athletics, and no one was near to hear Manuel call:

"Buck! Come here, Buck! Let's go for a stroll!"

Manuel led him through the orchard. Buck pranced and danced along beside him, enjoying the luscious smell of apples ripening on the trees. He was surprised, but very pleased when Manuel didn't turn back in the orchard. They were to have a longer walk on this silvery moonlit night.

They came to a little railroad station known as College Park. It was a flag station near the estate. A strange man stood in front of it. But he wasn't strange to Manuel.

"Here is the dog I said I'd sell you," Manuel said to the stranger.

"You might wrap up the goods before you deliver them," the stranger said gruffly, and Manuel doubled a piece of stout rope around Buck's neck under the collar.

Buck's long hair began to bristle. He was too proud to wear such a rope! His eyes began to darken as Manuel reached out his hand and took money from the stranger — but already it was too late.

A moment later, the gardener was gone. The stranger stood holding

on to Buck with a clutch that tightened the rope and almost shut off his breath. Buck, in quick rage, sprang at the man, who met him halfway.

He grappled him close by the throat and with a deft twist threw Buck down on his back. Again Buck struggled in fury, but the rope tightened mercilessly, and his tongue lolled out of his mouth. Never in all his life had he been treated so vilely! And never in all his life had he been so angry!

But still again that rope was tightened. Buck's strength suddenly ebbed and his eyes began to glaze. He could almost feel himself going unconscious. Then at last he knew nothing.

Nearby a locomotive whistled. The train was flagged. Two men from a baggage car jumped down and took hold of him.

Buck could neither know nor care. Manuel had trapped him. Like an evil thief in the night, he had started him on a mysterious journey. Already threatening winds seemed blowing from the frozen North.

11

Buck Goes To Sea

AGAIN the locomotive shrieked. From somewhere in the clutch of a nightmare, Buck vaguely heard the whistle. Slowly he opened his eyes.

He felt the train rolling on the tracks and sensed where he was. He was riding in a baggage car! He knew this because he had often traveled from place to place with Judge Miller. On those occasions he had been happy. Sometimes the Judge would come from the club car to see that things were all right with him. Often he had come from the dining car, too, bringing Buck chicken or steak in a paper napkin.

No kindly Judge came to see him now. He had scarcely opened his eyes when a stranger sprang at his throat. Again unbridled anger seized Buck. He started to his feet with the fury of a kidnaped king.

As fast as he was, he was still too late. The stranger was too quick for him. Although Buck's jaw closed on the hand that was skillfully choking him, he felt his breath cut off again. He was forced back into unconsciousness.

He didn't even hear the voice of a trainman who had come from another car to see what the struggle was about.

"What is happening here?" he asked Buck's captor.

"This dog has fits," the man said, hiding his mangled hand from the trainman. "I'm takin' him up for the boss to 'Frisco. A crack dog-doctor there thinks that he can cure him."

So the struggle between man and dog lasted all through the night.

The next day Buck was taken to a little shed in San Francisco. There he was delivered to still another tormentor. And the man from the baggage car grumbled:

"So all I get is fifty dollars for bringing this beast here! I wouldn't do it over again for a thousand!"

His hand was wrapped in a bloody handkerchief. He still seemed to feel the bite of Buck's sharp teeth. One trouser leg was ripped all the way down from his knee to his ankle.

"How much did the gardener get for kidnaping him from the Judge?" the new man asked the stranger.

"A hundred dollars," he grumbled again. "He wouldn't take anything less."

The new tormentor looked at Buck who was now on his feet attempting to face them. Stepping away from him warily, this new captor said:

"That makes a hundred and fifty dollars, but look at this dog from head to toe! He carries himself like a king, and from what you tell me, he can fight like a wild beast!" As Buck started toward him, he added, "This is the kind of dog we need in the North!" His eyes were frightened as Buck let out a long low growl. "Help me put him into this crate before you go," he ordered.

Buck's companion of the baggage car saw the look in Buck's eyes and whimpered:

"We'll both get hydrophobia!"

Buck let out a snarl as both men leaped upon him. Still dazed from his night in the baggage car, he was suffering unbearable pain. His tongue hurt, his throat was bruised, and the life was half-throttled out of him.

Once more he tried to face his captors, but it was two against one. He was thrown down and choked again until they at last succeeded in filing the heavy brass collar off his neck. After that, the rope was removed. Then Buck was roughly flung into a crate that was barred like a cage.

He lay there the rest of the weary night. He was full of wrath and wounded pride. He could not understand what all this meant. What did

14

these strangers want with him? Why were they keeping him pent up in this narrow crate? Buck did not know why, but he sensed more trouble was coming.

Several times during the night he heard the door of the shed open. Once he sprang to his feet, expecting to see Judge Miller coming here to get him. He almost started to bark with joy, but when he saw that it was only his captor, the bark turned into a savage growl.

Later four men came into the shed. They picked him up, crate and all, and carried him out to another train. Then he began to be passed through many strange hands. Clerks in an express office took charge of him and he was put into a wagon. This was met by a truck piled high with boxes and parcels. Poor Buck was put on top of them and the truck rolled away to a ferryboat.

Presently a whistle blew and he was taken off the ferry. He saw a strange railway depot and shuddered. He knew that every mile he went was taking him farther and farther away from his beautiful home in the Santa Clara valley. He felt his crate being picked up again. Finally he was put on a fast express train.

15

For two long days it shrieked along bright shining rails. Buck ate no food. He drank no water. He did not mind the hunger so much, but the lack of water caused him to suffer. This fanned his wrath to fever pitch.

But Buck was glad for one thing. The rope had not been put back upon his neck. Never, never, he vowed with bloodshot eyes, would he ever let them rope him again!

He heard a trainman calling, "Seattle." He was taken off the express train and new trouble started. Here was another strange tormentor. A MAN IN A RED SWEATER. AND HE CARRIED A BIG CLUB.

"I am here to break this red-eyed devil," this stranger said cruelly.

Right then and there began a whole new series of tortures such as Buck had never dreamed of. He was suddenly transformed into a raging fiend. Even the Judge would not have known him.

When his senses came back to him, he knew he was beaten, but not broken. He had learned, once and for all, that he stood no chance against a man with a club. It was his first meeting with primitive law and it aroused all the cunning in his nature.

At last the man in the red sweater surprised him. He brought Buck food and drink. The famished dog ate and drank eagerly. His instinct told him that he must, if he were ever to get strong enough to fight this enemy.

But the struggle between them was over. The man in the red sweater was approached by another swarthy fellow.

"How much do you want for that dog?" he asked.

"Three hundred dollars," said his captor, "and he's a steal at that."

"Looks like a wonderful dog," said this newest of strangers, and Buck saw money pass between them.

Again he was in strange new hands. Again he was starting a new journey. Presently he found himself on a ship at sea.

Strange New Masters And Companions

Buck's new masters were French-Canadians who had come down from the snowy Klondike. They worked for the Canadian Government, carrying mail by dog sled along the Yukon Trail.

Good dogs were needed to carry the mail. There were usually ten to a team. That was the reason these men had come down from the North to Seattle. They had to buy good dogs to work with. The short one answered to the name of Perrault. The big, dark-haired giant of a fellow was Francois.

Perrault knew dogs well. He looked at Buck and thought:

"This dog is one in a thousand! No," he went on, speaking aloud, "Buck is one dog in a million!"

Sea foam was washing the hull of the ship which was called the *Narwhal*. Buck had been led on shipboard by Perrault and then turned over to Francois. Buck was surprised to see another dog on deck — a big, good-natured female Newfoundland with the gentle brown eyes of a puppy. Francois called her Curly.

17

From the deck of the ship, across a blue expanse of water, Buck and Curly had their last glimpse of Seattle. It was the last time, too, that they were to feel the warm winds of this land that lay far south of the frozen North.

Buck and Curly were taken below deck by Francois. Both he and Perrault seemed new kind of men to Buck. While they commanded obedience from every dog in their keeping, they didn't seem cruel like the man in the baggage car, or the one in the red sweater.

Buck sensed that he would learn to respect these new masters, but he could give them no love. Love was a thing of the heart, and Buck's heart was still in the green fields of the Santa Clara Valley.

Somehow, he knew, though, that Perrault and Francois would be fair in their judgment of dogs. They would not play favorites with them. They would know how to handle them justly.

Now down below deck, Buck suddenly turned to look candidly at Curly. Curly wagged her tail and came up closer to Buck, as though she were saying:

"We are in this together, so we ought to be friends."

For a brief moment they nuzzled each other, then they were joined by other dogs. One was snow-white. He was a big strong fellow who had been owned by the captain of a whaling ship. He had a rather smiling face, but in an underhand way. Buck was to find this out in a hurry.

Francois was coming to feed the dogs. It was their first meal on shipboard and each dog was served in a separate dish. The snow-white dog gulped down his meat like a savage. Half-smiling, then, he walked toward Buck. Quick as a flash he stole Buck's bone.

Buck turned ferocious eyes on him and leaped in his direction. But even before he could make contact, Francois' whip came singing down on the white dog's back. Then he said quietly:

"It's your bone, Buck. Pick it up!"

Buck took the bone from right in under the white dog's nose. Yes, he had been right, his instinct was telling him. Francois would not coddle a dog, but he would be fair. Buck's respect for this new master grew.

He was munching on his bone when Perrault walked toward them, bringing still another dog. Buck eyed him intelligently. This one was a surly beast who answered to the name of Dave.

From the moment he joined them, he seemed to be making it clear that he wanted no part of any dog in the group. All he really wanted was to be left alone. He seemed to want only to eat and sleep and would take no interest in anything. He didn't even care what happened to them.

The *Narwhal* was crossing Queen Charlotte Sound. It rolled and pitched and tossed up and down like a ship possessed of a demon. Buck and Curly grew excited, then suddenly went half-wild with fear. This wasn't a ship, they were thinking! This thing they were on was as frail as a cobweb compared to this raging sea! Surely they'd all be drowned!

Buck began to fidget and Curly started to whimper. Dave raised his shaggy head and gave them both a disgusted look.

"Let us drown, for all I care," he seemed to be saying. "What have we got to lose?"

Then he yawned unsympathetically and went promptly back to sleep.

The *Narwhal* made the crossing safely. Day after day the ship plowed on through seas now calm, now rolling. But when the dogs were walked on deck, it was clear to Buck that the weather was steadily growing colder. Often he tried to make Curly run along the deck with him to get warm.

Then suddenly one morning Buck awakened with a start. He seemed to sense excitement all around him. The other dogs seemed to share it. The white one was sitting on his haunches, looking around inquiringly. The strong white dog was not even interested in stealing Buck's food.

Curly, in her Newfoundland way, was stretched out with her paws in front of her looking with big eyes at Buck, who now stood up and hurried forward to the cabin door.

Buck could not account for the excitement. The ship was still plowing doggedly on, but suddenly Buck's ears went up. Everything seemed instantly quiet! The ship's propeller had stopped! And Francois was coming toward them with leashes in his hands.

"Well, Buck," he half-smiled as the dog seemed almost questioning: "What is happening, Francois?"

The swarthy French-Canadian put the leash upon his collar.

"I've got something to show you," he whispered amiably in Buck's ear.

Then he and all the dogs and Perrault went up on deck and down a gangplank. Even at the top of it, Buck stopped in surprise. What strange new world was he coming to?

Silvery white flecks of something were falling down from the sky. There was no mud or grass to walk on, and the ground was white! He walked across it gingerly. It was cold! He sprang backward with a snort.

More of this white stuff was falling through the air. Buck shook himself, but still more fell upon him. He sniffed at it curiously — then licked some up with his tongue. It bit like fire! And the next instant, it was gone! This puzzled him. He tried to eat it again while Francois laughed aloud.

At the sound of his laughter, Buck straightened up and lifted his beautiful face to the sky.

The white stuff fell all over him. It sparkled like silvery stars.

This was Buck's first snow.

The Law Of The Club And Fang

BUCK was still blinking at the snow. Then he was made to realize more surprises were to come. He heard Francois say that they were on Dyea Beach. Buck would always remember that name with horror.

This was where he was to learn the terrible law of club and fang. There was no lazy sun-kissed life here. All was action and confusion. Life and limb were in deadly peril. There was a great need to be constantly alert, because the dogs and men here were not like those he had always known. These were like savages.

Buck had never seen dogs fight as these creatures fought. They were more like wolves than dogs. He and Curly stood stiff and stalwart, wondering how they might cope with them. They were called "Huskies" and there were more than a score. Both Buck and Curly were glad when Francois came and led them along the beach to a camp near a store built out of logs.

But Buck was to learn they should not have been glad. The snarling pack of Huskies followed. Then what happened made Buck freeze with terror. Big gentle Curly, in a friendly Newfoundland way, advanced to one of the Huskies. He was the size of a full-grown wolf, though not half so large as she.

22

"Woof! Woof!" Curly wagged her tail and seemed to be saying. "Surely we can be friends!"

Suddenly, without one sign of warning, Buck saw the snarling Husky leap! There was a furry clash in the air, a baring of teeth, and Curly's face was ripped, from her eyes down to her jaw.

"Curly!" If Buck could have talked, the name would have instantly come from his throat, but all he could do was to give a shrill bark.

Then Curly saw what he saw. These dogs not only looked like wolves. They had the wolf-manner of fighting! Thirty or forty ran to the spot where Curly and the Husky were still striking, body against body. They surrounded them in a circle — silent and intent. At first, Buck didn't understand why they were licking their chops and waiting — waiting —

Curly rushed to the Husky again, who struck her quickly, then leaped aside. He met her next movement with his chest, and in a peculiar fashion, tumbled her off her feet. And poor Curly lay there — never able to stand up again —

This, then, Buck realized was what the Huskies were waiting for. Savagely they all closed in. Yelping and snarling, they crushed her under the weight of their wild attack. Buck heard her give a scream of agony. Then gentle Curly's blood seeped out upon the snow.

It had happened so suddenly and unexpectedly that Buck was taken aback. Curly was dead and he, the strong one, had not been able to help her. The brutal attack of these savage strangers had been too swift and sure.

So *this* was the way a dog had to fight in this Northland! There was no fair play among them. No fair play at all. Once you went down, that was the end of you. The whole howling pack made sure of that. Well, thought Buck, I MUST NEVER GO DOWN! NEVER! NEVER! NEVER! What had happened to Curly would come back, he knew, to haunt him in his dreams. Curly had been the only one he had been close to since he had been kidnaped from the Santa Clara Valley.

"No, I must never go down," Buck told himself again.

He turned away from the sad scene to see Spitz, the mean white dog who would pay no attention to any of them, come up behind him. He, too, was watching the wolflike Huskies put an end to Curly, but he looked as though he was laughing. He was putting out his tongue and Buck saw that he was as untouched by Curly's tragedy as if it were nothing. Nothing at all. Buck could scarcely bear it.

From this moment on, he hated Spitz bitterly. He was about to make this clear to Spitz when he heard Francois calling:

"Get away from all this now, Buck. You are going to be harnessed."

Francois knelt down beside him in the snow. He fastened an arrangement of straps and buckles around Buck's body. It was a harness such as he had

seen the grooms put on horses at home. With a shock he realized that he was being made into a draft animal. He, Buck, the king!

"Now," said Francois, not unkindly, "we are going out to the forest and bring back a load of firewood."

Buck was too wise a dog to rebel. He fully realized now that the laws of this frozen land were different from any he had ever known. If he wanted to survive, he must learn to obey these laws. So he buckled down with a will and did his best, though it was all new and strange.

And he was not the only dog harnessed to pull Francois' sled. Dave was harnessed, too, and the hated Spitz, who seemed to be the leader. They were to pull the sled as a team.

They started off to run across the shining snow. Francois was stern. He demanded instant obedience. If he didn't get it, he used his whip. Dave, who like Spitz, had been harnessed before, nipped Buck's hind-quarters when he made a move that was wrong. And Spitz, even though he was leading the team, growled at Buck now and then or cunningly threw his weight in the traces to jerk Buck back into the way he should go.

Yes, he was whipped by Francois, nipped by Dave, and jerked around by the hated Spitz. Still Buck moved with dignity. Still he sensed that he must walk like a king. He must do this because he knew that he must become a king up here just as he used to be king of all he surveyed on Judge Miller's place in the Santa Clara Valley. Buck was that kind of dog.

He was learning to pull the sled along with the team very easily. The evergreen forest waved like green plumes in front of them. Francois stopped the sled and went to gather firewood.

Even before they got back to camp, Buck had learned his first lesson well. He knew when Francois said, "Ho!" he was supposed to stop. When he said "Mush!" he was to go — to swing wide on the bends of the snow path and to keep clear of the wheeler when the loaded sled shot down hill at their heels.

When they swung back into the camp on the beach, Francois called to Perrault:

"These are three vair' good dogs! Dat Buck pulls a sled like an expert! I teech him quick as anything!"

"Buck's one dog in a thousand!" Perrault had words of praise.

All traces of Curly, the lovely, friendly Newfoundland were gone. Not even a Husky was in sight. Buck mourned for Curly in his heart. He, too, could have made the same mistake.

One dog in a thousand!

"I have to be such a dog," sensed Buck, "or, I, too, will not live. This is the land where there is only one law. The law of the club and fang!"

Off To The Yukon!

PERRAULT was turning to two new dogs he had just brought back to camp. Billie and Jo, he called them. They were brothers and true Huskies both. Although the sons of one mother, they were as different as day and night. Billie was good-natured to a fault. Jo was quite the opposite. He greeted everyone with a snarl and an evil eye.

Buck met these dogs in tolerant fashion. Dave ignored them. Mean-hearted Spitz thrashed them both. And then, that evening, Perrault brought another dog to camp.

He was called Sol-leks, which means The Angry One. He was an old Husky, long and lean and gaunt. He had a battle-scarred face and only one eye. Like Dave, he asked nothing, gave nothing, expected nothing. But when he marched slowly into their midst, he flashed a warning of strength that commanded their respect. Even Spitz let him alone.

27

He had one peculiarity which Buck was unlucky enough to discover. Sol-leks did not like to be approached on his blind side. When innocent Buck first did this, Sol-leks whirled around upon him and slashed his shoulder to the bone. Forever after, Buck avoided his blind side, and to the last of their comradeship, had no more trouble.

But another problem came to Buck that night. It was — how to sleep? Francois' tent was pitched on the snowy beach. There was a candle glowing inside. It looked so warm and comfortable that Buck walked through the tent flap. Francois and Perrault were inside, but the moment they saw him, they growled. Francois hurled pots and pans at him. Turning ignominiously, Buck fled back into the cold.

A wintry wind was blowing in from a churning sea. It nipped him sharply and hurt his wounded shoulder. He lay down in the snow and tried to sleep, but the frost drove him shivering to his feet. Miserable and sad, he wandered about among other tents, but one place was as cold as another. Savage dogs rushed toward him, but he faced them masterfully. He bristled his neck-hair and snarled and they let him go his way.

Finally he had an idea. He would go back and see how his teammates were doing. Quickly he walked back to Francois' tent. He was surprised to find that all the dogs had disappeared. Were they in the tent, he wondered? But they couldn't be, he decided. He, alone, would not have been put out. Buck's tail drooped and he shivered again. He felt very forlorn.

Suddenly a strange thing happened. The snow gave way beneath his feet and he sank down. Something wiggled under his paws. He sprang back, bristling and snarling, fearful of the unknown. Then all at once he heard a friendly little yelp! He went back to investigate. A whiff of warm air ascended to his nostrils, and there, curled up under the snow in a snug little ball of fur, lay Billie!

He whined and squirmed to show his good intentions. He even put out his pink tongue to try and lick Buck's face. Buck nuzzled him softly and then he sensed:

"So this is the way they do it! They sleep under the snow so they can keep warm!"

Then, he, too, selected a spot and proceeded to dig a hole for himself. Quickly the heat from his body filled the space with warmth and he fell asleep.

The day had been long and hard. He slept now, soundly and comfortably, but sometimes he growled and barked and struggled with bad dreams. But he had learned another lesson — how to sleep in this Northland.

He did not open his eyes till roused by the noises of the waking camp. At first he didn't know where he was. It had snowed during the night and he was completely buried! Snow walls pressed him on every side. He was suddenly afraid. The great fear of the wild thing — the fear of being trapped.

This was a sign that Buck was remembering ancient instincts. He was harking back through his own life to the lives of his forebears. But Buck, of course, couldn't know this. He was a civilized dog and he had never

been trapped. How could he know that whatever was ancient in his blood was truly warning him now?

He only knew that the muscles of his whole body were contracting spasmodically and instinctively. The hair on his neck and shoulders stood up on end. Then with a sudden wild snarl he bounded out from the hole into the light of day.

He landed on his feet and saw the camp spread out before him. He remembered the beach. He remembered the nearby sea. He knew where he was and remembered even all that had passed from the time he went for a walk with Manuel, the gardener, to the hole he had dug for himself last night.

Suddenly he heard Francois shouting. Buck hailed his appearance by leaping from the hole and barking.

"Wot I say?" the dog driver cried to Perrault. "Dat Buck for sure learns queek as anything!"

Perrault nodded gravely. As courier for the Canadian Government, bearing important dispatches, he was always anxious to secure the best dogs available. He was particularly glad that he had Buck. He know how many long and dangerous journeys lay ahead for him and Francois and their team of dogs.

Three more Huskies were added to the team inside an hour, making a total of nine. In another quarter of an hour they were all in harness. Buck wondered where they were going now, but he was glad to be leaving.

This Dyea Beach had been a wild and savage place.

He remembered Curly and his eyes grew very gentle. It was as though he were telling her good-by.

"Curly," he mourned, almost aloud, "you are gone and I will miss you." Then, as he looked at the spot where she had last lain, something ferocious took hold of him. "I will learn to conquer this bitter land," he vowed to himself, "and when I do, I'll remember Curly, who had yet to learn the cruel law of the club and fang!"

So he stood with the team as Francois came toward them. Francois seemed to be in a specially good humor. He was smiling and snapping his whip in the air.

The restless dogs moved in harness. Metal bells upon their collars made a ringing sound.

Francois took his place on the sled as the dog driver. Again he curled his whip above his head.

"Mush!" he called to the dog team. "We are off to the Yukon!"

A Leader Must Lead!

BUCK was surprised at the eagerness which seemed to overtake the whole team. All the dogs were impatient to be on their way. Even Dave and Sol-leks, who were new to the harness, seemed to welcome pulling the sled across the snow.

"Mush!" This command from Francois was a challenge to them all.

Each dog was alert and anxious to do his bit. He wanted the work to go well and was annoyed if it did not. The toil of the traces seemed to be a thing of delight.

"Mush!" It was Francois' voice again.

All the dogs rushed forward, as if the snowy unknown ahead was a high, clear call to them.

Dave was the wheeler or sled dog. Pulling in front of him was Buck. Then came Sol-leks and the rest, strung out ahead, single file, straight up to the leader, Buck's hated rival, Spitz.

Buck looked over the heads of the other dogs and snarled a mighty snarl. It was as though he was saying:

"You may be the leader now, but you will not be for long. I am going to take your place!"

32

He did not realize yet that he had been purposely placed between Dave and Sol-leks so that he might receive instruction. They were to teach him how to run in the trace, even if they had to use their teeth.

Dave was fair and very wise. He never nipped Buck without cause, but he did nip him if he had to. And Francois' whip backed him up. During a brief halt, when Buck got tangled in the traces, both Dave and Sol-leks flew at him. They would not stand for such nonsense, delaying the whole team!

He felt the blows of their sound trouncing. Then he got tangled even worse and both dogs went at him again. After that, Buck took good care to keep the traces clear.

By the end of the first day, Buck was to master his work so well that his mates would stop nagging him. Francois would cease to use his whip and Perrault would even honor Buck by lifting up his feet, one by one, and carefully examining them for bruises.

"We don't want to hurt you, Buck," said Perrault.

It was a hard day's work up the Canon through Sheep Camp, past the Scales, and on to the timber line. They crossed glaciers and snow drifts hundreds of feet deep. Then over the great Chilcoot Divide they went doggedly. It stood between the salt water and the fresh, guarding the sad and lonely North like a sleeping giant.

So this was the wonderful Yukon Trail! And even though the dangers of it were many, Buck and all the other dogs felt a thrill in their hearts to be running it. They made good time down a chain of lakes which filled the craters of extinct volcanoes. That night they came to Lake Bennett.

Here the meaning of the Gold Rush was really unfolded before Buck's eyes. Thousands and thousands of gold seekers were here. They came from every walk of life to search for a golden stream of wealth. Adventurers all — men and women both — sometimes whole families.

Buck and the team had made forty miles that day. He and the other dogs were exhausted. They dug themselves holes deep in the snow and slept the sleep of the just. Then, all too early, they were called — routed out into cold darkness — and harnessed to the sled again.

Buck was quick to notice the difference in the trail. The first day it had been already packed. Today they had to break their own, work harder, and make poorer time. Perrault, as a rule, traveled ahead most of the time, packing the snow with webbed snowshoes to make it easier for the team. Francois, guiding the sled at the gee-pole, sometimes exchanged places with him, but not often. Perrault was in a hurry and he prided himself on his knowledge of ice.

Day after day, for days unending, Buck toiled in the traces. Up before dawn. No rest until long after dark. And always, always the dogs were hungry! Each one was rationed. Buck's share was a pound and a half of dried salmon which seemed to go nowhere.

He was not the dainty eater he had been at Judge Miller's. He knew that he had to eat as fast as he could or the other dogs would finish first, then fight for his food. He was learning to be as they were under the law of club and fang.

His progress was fast. His muscles became as hard as iron. He was growing callous to all ordinary pain. He could eat anything and digest it. His sight and scent became remarkably keen, while his hearing became so good that even in his sleep he could hear the faintest sound. And he knew whether it meant peace or peril.

He learned to bite ice out with his teeth when it collected between his toes. When he was thirsty and there was thick scum over a water hole, he learned how to break it by rearing and striking it with stiff front legs. Yes, Buck was learning how to do things in order to live in this wild and cold land.

The bloodline of his ancient ancestors was very strong in Buck. Under the fierce conditions of life on this open trail it began to make itself felt more and more every day. And the newborn cunning he was feeling gave him poise and control. But not until that fateful day when the great urge overcame him did he really know how strong he had become.

As always, when he looked at Spitz, his eyes betrayed his bitter hatred. Dog, in fact, measured dog, and each one knew by instinct that a clash must one day come between them. It was as though Buck told himself:

"A leader must lead and I am a leader! Spitz is the one who must go!"

The Combat Is On

BUCK's cunning was so highly developed now that he started a campaign against the lead-dog, Spitz. He sensed that he could threaten his leadership. When open warfare came, as he knew it must, he would be ready.

One night in camp he made his nest under a sheltering rock. It was so snug and warm that he hated to leave it, even when Francois called him to supper. He was so very hungry, though, that he got out of his nest to eat the fish that Francois had thawed over the campfire. Then Buck sauntered back to his shelter, only to find it occupied. The hated Spitz had curled up in his nest!

The lead-dog gave a warning snarl. The beast in Buck roared. This was the time to bring their fight out into the open! He sprang upon Spitz with a fury that surprised the lead-dog. Spitz had rarely felt that Buck would actually attack him!

Spitz shot from the sheltering nest, all fang and claws and fury. He, indeed, was the leader here! How could this upstart dare to question that?

Francois was standing nearby and made no gesture to stop them.

"Gif it to heem, Buck," he cried. "Make him give you back your nest! He is a dirty thief!"

Buck circled back and forth around the lead-dog in rage. He was skillfully hedging for the advantage. Then something unexpected happened which ended not only Buck's action, but Spitz's. Both dogs heard a terrible yowl. Then a cry from Perrault:

"Get into action, Francois! We're being attacked by mad dogs!"

Then Buck saw what Francois saw. Forty or fifty wild dogs had crept into the camp in search of food. They were actually crazy with hunger. They tore toward the grub-box like a herd of famished wolves.

Perrault and Francois attacked them with clubs. The dogs were so hungry that the clubs might just as well have been matches! Then as the team-dogs started to bark, the famished horde set upon them.

Buck had never seen such dogs. They were as bony as skeletons. Both he and Spitz had to forget that they had been fighting each other and fight to protect themselves. From that moment on, the whole camp was a scene of violence and blood. Three Huskies set on Buck. His head and shoulders were ripped and slashed. The other team dogs fared no better.

Buck was goaded to greater fierceness. Then suddenly he saw the hated Spitz take a flying leap in his direction. Spitz, the mean and treacherous one, was now attacking Buck instead of the wild dogs! He knew that if he could throw Buck off his feet, the yelling, starving horde would devour him.

Buck braced himself for Spitz's charge. He was able to stand his ground. He would not let Spitz throw him over! With a snarl right in the very face of Spitz, Buck made a leap that sent him flying. Then he turned to help his masters fight the wild dogs in their midst.

Perrault and Francois were proud of him. When they had at last routed the Huskies with huge clubs, they rounded up their team. There was not one who was not wounded in four or five places. Others were injured grievously. Buck's hide was so badly torn, it hung in loose shreds.

Francois shook his head sadly as he examined him.

"You were one beeg hero, Buck," he said. "Some of these dogs ran away, but you stayed here to fight." He turned to Perrault who was examining the other dogs. "I hope none have wounds that will drive them mad. Wot you think, Perrault?"

The courier shook his head. Even he couldn't tell what would be the outcome. He only knew that there were still four hundred miles of the trail between this place and Dawson, where they had to go.

It took much patience and two hours to get the dog-team back in harness. Painfully they began to struggle over the hardest part of the trail they had yet encountered.

Nothing daunted Perrault, it seemed to Buck. That was why he had been chosen to be a government courier. But even he was most discouraged when the next day brought more trouble. Dolly, one of the team-dogs, went mad.

It was the first time Buck had ever seen a dog go through this experience. Suddenly Dolly gave a call, a long, heartbreaking howl. It made every dog on the sled-team bristle with fear. Then, suddenly, too, she sprang straight for Buck.

He fled away from her in panic. He could hear her snarling just one leap behind him. And out of the corner of his eye, he saw Francois following them. He had a big, sharp-edged axe in his hand. Francois called to Buck but already he had gone a quarter of a mile. Hearing the call, he doubled back with Dolly still at his heels.

"Buck! Buck! Over here!" Francois was commanding.

Blindly Buck obeyed him. He saw that Francois was standing near the empty sled with the axe poised in his hand. Dolly's howls were yelps of terror as she kept on following Buck. Then, as he ran past the dog-sled, Francois threw the axe with skill. It put Dolly out of her misery. She lay dead upon the snow.

Buck staggered over against the sled. He was exhausted and sobbing for breath. Immediately new trouble started. Spitz saw this opportunity. Now, he sensed, he could really kill Buck! Attack him while he was helpless! Savagely he sprang upon the weary dog. He tore Buck's flesh to the bone.

Meanwhile Buck heard an angry cry. He saw Francois curl his whip high in the air. Then he felt Spitz's teeth release him as the whip came down upon Spitz's back.

"You devil, Spitz!"cried Francois. "Some day you will kill dat Buck! You jealous, huh?"

Buck saw him give Spitz a whipping such as he had never given any dog on this sled-team.

Perrault watched it all calmly. He felt, too, that Spitz should be punished for his treachery. Then finally he spoke:

"Don't be too sure that Spitz will kill Buck," he told Francois. "Some fine day, I warn you, Buck will chew him up! Sure thing! I know!"

And Spitz, now free from Francois, faced Buck with glaring eyes. Then he turned away and ran into a hole. He and Buck both knew now it was war between them.

One Is Triumphant

"**A** LEADER must lead and I am a leader!"

This instinctive sense of strength seemed to overpower Buck. His nature had been gripped now by his pride in toil and the trace.

He had come to learn that it was pride that kept all these sled dogs in the harness. This was the pride of Dave, as wheel dog, of Sol-leks, as he pulled with all his strength. It was the same pride which makes dogs toil to the last gasp, which lures them to die joyfully in the harness and breaks their hearts if they are put off the team.

This was the pride that bore up Spitz and made him thrash the other dogs when they sometimes made a mistake. And it was this pride, too, that made Spitz fear that Buck would try and take his place as leader.

"A leader must lead and I am a leader!"

This was what Buck was waiting for. This was what he must accomplish.

Through combat after combat, both dogs rose to the challenge. No opportunity came for a real showdown before they pulled into Dawson. Dawson in the Klondike! The center of the gold mining region! It was something for Buck to see!

Everywhere there was life and color. The Royal Canadian Mounted Police — "Mounties," people called them — rode down the streets on beautiful horses that stepped high with pride. Their red coats seemed alive with color. Gold braid and gold buttons on them glistened.

People who sought gold crowded narrow streets. In and out of shops and hotels they came and went — the search for gold gleaming in their eyes.

And then there were the dogs. Buck had never seen so many at work as there were in Dawson. All day they swung up and down the main street in long teams. Even in the night, Buck could hear bells jingling on their collars.

They hauled logs to build cabins and flatboats. They carried freight up to the gold mines and did all sorts of work that horses had done back in the Santa Clara Valley. Here and there Buck met a dog like himself who had been stolen from the Southland, but most of them were wild wolf breeds. And when their day's work was done, this is what they did:

Every night at nine o'clock, and then at twelve, and then at three, they chanted a weird song. Lifting their faces to the sky, they sang the song of the Huskies. Their long-drawn wails and pleading sobs brought strange lumps to many men's throats.

And Buck was affected by this song. He, too, lifted his face to the sky, aglow with northern lights. He, too, without quite knowing why, moaned and sobbed along with the savage Huskies. He, too, felt the urge of ancient calls deep within his bloodlines. The call of the wild, Buck. THE CALL OF THE WILD!

He did not realize this was what it was. After he had chanted, he settled back into the traces.

It took Perrault a week to accomplish his mission in Dawson. Then, with more important papers than he had ever carried before, he started back on the Yukon Trail, headed for Dyea Beach.

And it was on this homeward trek that the great moment came. Spitz spied a snowshoe rabbit. It was big and beautiful and white, scarcely visible on the snow. Spitz went after it, making a kill. Then, as the rabbit gave a last and terrified shriek, all the dogs on the team headed for the spot.

Buck went flying with them. He drove upon Spitz, shoulder to shoulder. Such was the rage in both dogs' eyes that the other dogs stood back. They stood in a circle and watched Buck fight Spitz to become their leader. This was the battle to the death and all the sled dogs knew it.

Spitz was a great fighter. From Spitzbergen through the Arctic, across Canada and the Barrens, he had held his own with all manner of dogs and had mastered them. He never rushed until he was prepared to receive a rush. He never attacked until he had first defended that attack.

Buck tried to sink his teeth into this big white dog. Time and time again he aimed at his throat, but Spitz stood his ground. He would drive his shoulder at the shoulder of Spitz, as a ram to overthrow him. Instead, Buck's shoulder was slashed and Spitz would leap lightly away. He was untouched, while Buck was streaming with blood and panting hard.

"I am a leader and a leader must lead!"

The chant in his mind was as wild as the song he had sobbed with the Huskies in Dawson. It drove him on to attack again and again. And once he nearly went down on his back.

"I am a leader and a leader must lead!"

Buck had a quality that made for greatness and it was imagination. In spite of his wounds, instinctively now, his teeth closed on Spitz's left front leg. It was broken to the bone, but Spitz still faced him on three.

Again Buck charged and repeated the trick on Spitz's right front leg. Still Spitz struggled madly, but he knew that his cause was lost. There was no hope for him now. He could not fight on only two legs. Buck had almost won. He was maneuvering for the kill.

Moonlight flooded the white, white snow. The struggling of the dogs made brutal shadows upon it. Spitz went down with a long, sad cry. Buck stood over him, triumphant.

Out of the savage reaches of these desolate snow lands, he seemed to hear a ringing song —

"I am a leader and a leader must lead!"

He turned back to the sled team. He walked like the king dog that he was. Yes, Buck had won by the law of this Northland. Now he was the leader of the team!

Weaklings And John Thornton

BUCK! His face was shining. He stood like a king against the glistening snow. Buck! Tall in the trace at the head of the team! Buck! This was his first day as leader!

Francois looked at him, glowing:

"Never such a dog as dat Buck!" he was saying to Perrault. "You were right about him, I say! Him worth more than a thousand dollars!"

Perrault, too, looked at Buck with respect. He looked fine and fit and strong as a savage wolf. Even the other dogs on the team seemed to look at him with pride. Then Perrault said:

"I told you he'd put an end to Spitz and now he has done it."

Perrault gave a teasing war-whoop and started off on the hard white trail. Francois called:

"Mush!"

When he cracked his whip in the cold, dry air, Buck started pulling. As if they stood as one, backing him solidly, the other dogs pulled, too. The Yukon Trail was in excellent condition. There was no new-fallen snow to worry about. Perrault was out to make a record and gaining every day. Now with Buck as the leader, and all the dogs working in unison, he had a good chance of making his goal.

The Thirty Mile River was coated with ice. They covered in one day what had taken them ten days to cover on their way to Dawson. They made a sixty-mile dash from the foot of Lake Le Barge to the White Horse Rapids. Across Marsh, Tagish, and Bennett — seventy miles of lakes — they ran so rapidly that the dogs felt they were flying. On the last night of the second week, they were on the top of White Pass, ready to drop down the sea-slope. Both men and dogs saw Skagway at their feet.

Every day for fourteen days they had averaged forty miles. Perrault had made a record run and was ready to shout with joy. He threw his fur gloves in the air:

"We've made it, Buck! We've made it!" he cried. "Everyone in town is talking about our run and our wonderful dogs! And you were the leader, Buck! You were the leader!"

Buck stood proudly looking ahead, but his tail was wagging. If he could have talked, he would have said:

"I'll make many runs with you and Francois. I am a leader and a leader must lead!"

He held his head high. His eyes glowed with pleasure.

But as it had come before, trouble was to come again. Perrault and Francois received certain official orders. They could not drive this sled again. Buck and the team would have to be sold.

Francois knelt beside him, weeping:

"I don't want to sell you, Buck. You are such a wonderful dog. I have learned to love you."

Buck turned his head and blinked. No more trips with Francois? No more running at the head of his team? A sorrow deep within him made Buck gulp hard. Francois and Perrault were passing out of his life.

A Scotch half-breed bought him and his teammates. In company with a dozen other dog teams, Buck started back over the weary trail to Dawson.

Buck did not like these strangers, but he was a leader and he had a code. So well did he perform that he became the master of all strange teams he had to work with, and not only his own. He was respected everywhere by both dogs and men.

But something else was happening. Buck was having queer dreams at night. Lying in front of the campfire, he blinked lazily at the flames. Sometimes he thought of Judge Miller and the Santa Clara Valley. Often he remembered the man in the red sweater who had been so cruel to him. And he remembered Curly, whom the wolflike Huskies had killed. And Spitz.

There was another dream, a new one. He seemed to be in a dark forest. There were shadows all around him and he thought he heard the chilling call of wolves. His hair would rise along his back. He would whimper low and growl. It was like being in another world. It seemed that he was waiting. Waiting for something or someone . . .

Sometimes the cook would shout at him good-naturedly. "Hey, you, Buck! Wake up! You dreaming!"

At the sound of his voice, the world of the shadowy forest would vanish. He would open his eyes to this real world of the snowy Yukon Trail and the sacks of mail to be delivered. So back and forth he led the team-dogs to Dawson. Then from Dawson back to Skagway. And then one day he was sold again.

Buck stood up stalwart and looked at his new masters. There were two men and a woman. They had a slipshod tent and a dirty dog sled. They were not mail train drivers, as Francois and Perrault had been, or even the Scotch half-breed. These people had come to the Klondike only to seek gold. Buck wanted to curl his lip at them. His instinct told him they were weaklings.

Now the worst of all times began for Buck. The men's names were Charles and Hal. The woman's name was Mercedes. They knew nothing at all about driving dogs. They didn't know how to pack a sled. They couldn't judge conditions of ice and snow. They scarcely knew when to come and go, but they did know how to beat their dogs.

One night they stopped to camp at White River. There was another camper there. His name was John Thornton. He warned them not to push on farther. Spring, he said, was coming with a rush. The ice could break at any time and put them and their dogs in peril.

Buck's instinct told him that this man was right. His masters should wait here for better weather. He made up his mind to lay down on the trail like a stubborn mule rather than put his teammates in danger. And when Buck laid down, all the other dogs did, too. All refused to budge.

His new master uncoiled his whip. He struck Buck like a savage.

"You, Buck! Get up! Mush! Mush!"

Still Buck refused to move a muscle. Hal beat him unmercifully. The lash cut into him like a knife. Blood ran in trickles down his poor sides.

John Thornton was a seasoned camper. He knew the ways of dogs and men. He saw these people were mere weaklings. Shaking with rage, he faced Buck's master:

"If you strike that dog again, I'll kill you," he cried.

But Hal went on lashing.

"He's my dog," he said, "and he's going to Dawson, ice or no ice."

John Thornton stood between him and Buck. Hal drew a long hunting knife from his belt, but still John Thornton protected Buck. Suddenly he made a move and knocked the knife out of Hal's hand with the handle of an axe he had been using.

Hal turned quite pale. This man, John Thornton, was not fooling. He would really kill him if he dared to strike Buck again! Silently he watched John Thornton stoop down. With one swift stroke he cut Buck's traces to set him free from the sled.

"You poor dog!" he was saying sympathetically. "He's almost beat you dead!"

Fearful of him and what he might do, Hal spoke a single word.

"Mush!" he cried to the other dogs.

Sorrowfully Buck half-raised his head as he heard them go. Pike was leading in his place. Sol-leks was at the wheel, and between were Joe and Tek. They were limping and staggering — too tired to move. Buck was too weak to look any longer. His head lolled back on the ground again.

John Thornton knelt on the snow beside him. His hands were rough and kindly. He searched Buck's body for broken bones.

By the time his search was over, Hal's sled was a quarter of a mile away. Both he and Buck watched it crawling along over the ice. Suddenly they saw it drop and heard awful screams. A whole section of ice had broken on the Yukon Trail and was burying them forever.

John Thornton looked down at Buck and stroked his head with a loving hand.

"You're left alone with me now, Buck," he said. "You are almost starved and there are ugly wounds — but you're my dog now — my dog!"

The soothing tenderness in his voice was such as Buck had never heard, even at Judge Miller's.

Feebly he tried to raise his head. Then he licked John Thornton's hand.

The Love Of John Thornton

JOHN THORNTON's feet had been frozen months before Buck had come to him. Friends who had been with him had made him a comfortable camp on the trail and then pushed on to Dawson. It was planned that he should join them there when he was able to travel.

He was still limping a little when he had rescued Buck, but he was strong and well. He taught Buck to laze through the long spring days. To watch the running water in the Yukon River. To listen to the song of birds that had come for a brief springtime in this frozen North.

Buck traveled three thousand miles. This rest was well-earned. His wounds slowly healed. His muscles swelled out. Flesh came back to cover his bones. And it was not only John Thornton who took such wonderful care of him. There were his two dogs, named Skeet and Nig. And they took such a fancy to Buck, they helped to make him well!

Skeet was a little Irish setter. She had a "doctor trait" which some dogs possess. As a mother cat washes her kittens, so Skeet washed and cleansed Buck's wounds, even when he was in a dying condition.

Regularly, each morning, after Buck had finished his breakfast, Skeet performed her self-appointed task. Buck came to look for her care as much as he did John Thornton's. Nig was a huge black dog, equally friendly, half-bloodhound, half-deerhound, with boundless good nature. Even his eyes seemed to laugh.

To Buck's surprise, neither Skeet nor Nig showed any jealously toward him. They seemed to share the same kindliness and gentleness that John Thornton had. As Buck grew stronger, they coaxed him to play all sorts of funny games. Often their master took part. Thus Buck romped through his getting-well days and into a new life such as he had never known.

49

Even in the Santa Clara Valley, Buck had been more of a protector of the whole family than attached to any one man. But here on the Yukon he had met the master he adored.

Other men took care of dogs from a sense of duty. John Thornton took care of them as though they were his children. He never forgot a kindly greeting or a cheering word. He would sit down for long talks with them with as much delight as if they were his best friends.

He had a way of taking Buck's head between his hands, resting his own head on Buck's, and murmuring funny little endearing words. Buck would stand quite still and listen with the deepest devotion. Then, when John Thornton released him, he would spring apart from him. His mouth would seem to laugh and his eloquent eyes almost said:

"You are the man who saved my life! I will love you forever!"

Once John Thornton exclaimed:

"Buck, oh, Buck, wonderful dog that you are! You can all but speak!"

Yes, Buck's love was adoration. He went wild with happiness when John Thornton touched him or spoke to him, but oddly enough, he did not seek these caresses. Skeet would shove her nose under John Thornton's hand and nudge and nudge until she was petted. Nig would stalk up and rest his great black head on John Thornton's knee. But Buck was content to adore from a distance.

He would lie by the hour at John Thornton's feet, looking up into his face. It seemed that he was studying it, following each changing expres-

sion. Sometimes he would lie a bit farther away and watch everything John Thornton did. Often Buck's looks were so compelling that John Thornton's eyes would be drawn to him. He would return Buck's gaze without even speaking, but it was as though his heart was shining out to Buck, as the dog's heart was shining out to him.

For a long time after Buck's rescue, he did not like John Thornton to get out of his sight. From the moment he left his tent to when he entered it again, Buck would follow at his heels. Because he had known so many masters in this Northland, his great fear was that no master would be permanent. He was afraid that John Thornton would pass out of his life, as Francois and Perrault and all the others had.

Sometimes in the night, he dreamed that John Thornton had gone away from him for good. Haunted by this fear, Buck would shake off sleep. Then, walking to the tent where his master lay, he would stand and listen to John Thornton's breathing.

"You are my master," Buck wanted to tell him. "We must never be parted!"

So John Thornton held his affection. The rest of mankind was as nothing. John Thornton owned Buck's whole heart.

Then one day Buck discovered something strange. His heart was one thing. His mind was another. He was having queer dreams again. At night he was off in a shadowy forest, waiting for a haunting call. . . . When morning came, and he woke up, John Thornton seemed dearer than ever.

For Love Of His Master

WHEN the ice was strong again, they pushed on to Dawson. Here, during the long winter nights, men sat in the gold-mining camps and talked about their dogs. Sometimes they bragged.

One man told the campers:

"My dog could start a sled loaded with four hundred pounds."

Then a second man said:

"Ho, is that all? My dog could start six hundred pounds!"

Buck was lying at John Thornton's feet. He saw his master look down at him.

"Pooh!" said John Thornton. "Buck can start a thousand pounds!"

All three men looked at him astonished. One named Matthewson said:

"And break it out, and walk off with it for a hundred yards?"

"And break it out, and walk off with it for a hundred yards," John Thornton repeated coolly.

"I'll bet you a thousand dollars he can't!" Matthewson challenged him.

Even Buck's ears went straight up. A THOUSAND DOLLARS! Why, that would buy the new equipment John Thornton needed. It would enable him to make a trip to a place far east of Dawson, where gold miners had not yet appeared.

John Thornton was standing up.

"I'll take your bet," he was saying to Matthewson. Then he turned to Buck, who started wagging his tail. "Come, Buck," he commanded.

Even while Buck followed him, John Thornton was uneasy. Perhaps these men had called his bluff! He did not know whether or not faithful Buck could start a thousand pounds. That was a whole half-ton! He had great faith in Buck's strength, but a sled loaded with a thousand pounds would be appalling to any dog in the world!

Nevertheless, preparations were made. And as Buck stood on the starting line, he felt excitement all around him. Every man in camp was watching. He must do what he had to do as a tribute to John Thornton!

His master knelt down beside him. He took Buck's head in his two hands and rested cheek on cheek. He did not play a game with him. He just whispered in his ear:

"As you love me, Buck. As you love me."

Buck whined with eagerness. As he loved his master? The man who had saved his life and so tenderly cared for him? He was so filled with devotion that he knew he would rather die than disappoint John Thornton.

Those who looked on almost held their breath. Then John Thornton's command to Buck rang out like a pistol shot.

"Mush, Buck! MUSH!"

Buck threw himself forward, tightening the traces with a jarring lunge. His whole body was gathered together in effort. His muscles were live things under his fur. His great chest was low to the ground. His masterful head was forward and down. And his feet were flying like mad, scarring the hard-packed snow.

The sled swayed and trembled, half-started forward. Then one of his feet slipped and one man groaned. Again Buck strained like a monster. Presently, in what looked like a succession of jerks, again the sled moved. An inch. Two inches. Then it gained speed and moved steadily along.

The onlookers gasped. Buck was moving a thousand pounds! Some of the men seemed hypnotized by the sight. John Thornton ran behind the sled, encouraging Buck with cheering words:

"Good Buck! Wonderful Buck! Oh, as you love me!"

A pile of firewood marked the spot where Buck was to stop. It was the end of the hundred yards set for him to make. And Buck, for love of John Thornton, made it.

"Stop now, Buck, stop!" John Thornton commanded.

Buck stood stock-still at the sound of a roar which went up from the crowd. Every man was cheering him. They threw their hats high in the air. Their mittens went flying. Yes, they had seen a wonderful thing — the love of a dog for his master. They could scarcely shout loud enough. Some were even shaking hands.

"Buck, oh, Buck!"

John Thornton fell down on his knees beside him. Again it was head against loving head, and he was shaking Buck back and forth.

Then one man in the crowd cried out:

"I'll give you a thousand dollars for that dog! No, twelve hundred!"

John Thornton looked him straight in the eye:

"Not all the gold in Dawson could ever buy Buck from me," he answered.

Buck seemed to know what he was saying. As John Thornton fondled him again, he half-raised up in the trace and put his two front paws gently on his master's shoulders.

Tears streamed down John Thornton's face. And he was not ashamed.

The Sounding Of The Call

AGAIN and again, Buck showed his love for his master, John Thornton. The next time it was in camp at Circle City.

Two men were standing near the campfire. One looked mean and ill-natured. The other was a tenderfoot. The mean one was Black Barton.

"Put some wood on the fire," he ordered the young stranger.

The stranger looked at him calmly. He had seen Black Barton order other young men around and he did not like it. He looked at the huge, black-bearded bully and said:

"If you want more wood on the fire, put it on yourself."

The huge giant of a fellow made an angry lunge toward the tenderfoot. Good-naturedly, then, John Thornton placed himself between them. And Buck, as was his custom, was lying nearby, watching his master.

"Please, Black Barton," John Thornton was saying, but this evil-tempered one would not let him finish.

He struck out, without warning, straight from the shoulder. John Thornton was sent spinning. He could scarcely save himself from falling.

Those looking on heard what was neither yelp nor growl, but an angry roar. They saw Buck's body rise up in the air as he left the floor for Black Barton's throat. The man saved his life instinctively by throwing out his arm, but was hurled backward to the floor with raging Buck on top of him.

Buck loosed his teeth from the flesh of the arm and drove in again for the throat — and this time — tore it open. Then, in great alarm, other campers burst in upon Buck, and he was driven off with clubs.

He prowled up and down, growling ferociously as a surgeon checked Black Barton. A "miner's meeting" was held on the spot — a court of trial — with Buck the prisoner. It lasted only a few minutes, then he was set free. Buck, they decided, had every right to try and protect his own master.

The dog's reputation was made. From that day on, Buck's name was known and honored in every gold-mining camp in Alaska.

Later on, in the fall of the year, he saved John Thornton's life in quite another fashion. His master was poling a boat down a bad stretch of rapids on Forty Mile Creek. His partners were watching him from the shore. Suddenly, they saw with horror that the boat was turning over. Seething, swirling waters were sucking John Thornton in!

At once the partners realized no man could fight against such currents and whirlpools. They could see John Thornton gasping for breath. Something must be done — and quickly!

But faithful Buck had heard his master gasping, too. He sprang to his feet and raced to the shoreline. Then suddenly he growled and showed his teeth as he felt four hands upon him, holding him back from jumping into the river. Briefly he listened to their soothing voices:

"You can't save your master unless you save yourself, Buck! Steady now — let us put this rope around you —"

They put the rope around his body, then around a tree. Meanwhile, they let Buck jump into the whirling stream. Once he tried to rescue his master, but he was beaten back and battered by the force of angry waters. A second time he tried. He was almost strangled and dragged over pointed rocks. But still, Buck tried again.

John Thornton was almost lifeless when Buck at last came swimming toward him. With a gasp he reached up and closed both arms around Buck's shaggy neck. Then he held on while they struggled against the wicked current. First one was uppermost in the water, then the other, both man and dog clasped together — clasped and determined to win.

And win they did, because Buck was brave. Scarcely had they reached the shore when he went unconscious. Yes, he was unconscious, but he had saved John Thornton's life!

Nig and Skeet came dashing forward. Nig started setting up a high

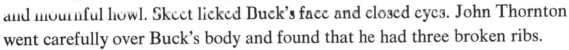

and mournful howl. Skeet licked Buck's face and closed eyes. John Thornton went carefully over Buck's body and found that he had three broken ribs.

"That settles it," he announced. "We camp right here until Buck's ribs have knitted and he is able to travel again."

It was weeks and weeks until they could take to the trail once more. Buck became well and strong — and, as it had always been — his heart was owned by good John Thornton. Then one night a strange thing happened. Buck had another dream.

Even in the depths of sleep he realized he was being called. Yes, something wanted him to come. He sprang up from his sleep with a start, eager-eyed, his nostrils quivering. And then he heard the voice again — a long-drawn howl — like, yet unlike, any noise made by a Husky dog. It seemed to come from the neighboring forest. Even though he had heard it in his dreams before, this call was, somehow, different.

Buck sprang through the sleeping camp. In silence he dashed off through the woods. As he drew closer to the cry, he went more slowly, caution in every movement. Suddenly he came to an open clearing.

He stopped short at the sight before him. There — erect on his haunches — nose pointed up to the sky — a long, lean timber wolf was howling.

Buck Gives His Answer

BUCK stalked into the open, half-crouching. His body was tightened together, his tail was straight and stiff. His feet were falling with extra care. It was a kind of half-truce approach made by beasts of prey.

But the wolf fled at the sight of him. Buck followed with wild leapings and a frenzy overtook him. In a short time he had cornered the wolf in a patch of timber. Then a very strange thing happened. Neither dog nor wolf wanted to attack! Somehow they felt they were friends.

Buck circled the wolf in a friendly manner. Plainly no harm was intended, so the wolf let Buck come close. Then suddenly they both sniffed noses. It was as though they had said:

"Perhaps we do belong together!"

They started playing like mischievous puppies, a way in which fierce beasts sometimes show they are not really fierce. Then, after a while, the wolf walked away, but he looked back over his shoulder, pleading:

"Come with me, Buck! Come!"

And so they both began to run. Side by side, under a sky the gray of twilight, they raced up a creek bed. Then down into a gorge they went and up the other side. Here they came to level country, green with great stretches of forest and sparkling with many streams. But they ran steadily on, hour after hour.

The sun rose higher and the day grew almost warm. Buck had never been so excited in his whole life. He knew he was at last answering the call. This wolf with yellow eyes was his own wood brother! It seemed to him that long ago, he had run this way. That he himself had been a wolf!

Still they kept on running. Free and wild, they were guided by an ancient call. And Buck was made to realize that this was where he had been in all those troubling dreams. Running free! Seeking his wood brother! And he was wildly glad!

They stopped beside a running stream to drink of its clear water. Only then did Buck remember wonderful John Thornton. Suddenly, he sat down. The wolf started on toward the place from which another call seemed to be coming. Then he came back to Buck and sniffed noses.

He was coaxing Buck to follow, but Buck's heart was taking over. He had to return to his master. He had to be faithful to John Thornton.

He started to backtrack through the forest. His master was eating dinner when he dashed up to him. His voice was filled with gladness when he said: "Buck, old fellow, where have you been?"

Buck sprang upon him in a frenzy of affection. He put his paws upon his master's broad shoulders — licked his face — and kissed his hands. John Thornton hugged Buck very close.

For two days and nights Buck never left camp. He wouldn't let John Thornton out of his sight. He followed him about at his work, watched him while he ate, saw him into blankets when he went to sleep at night. Then the great call came again. The clear call of the wild!

Buck could not resist it. He tore through the forest, but this time alone. He could not find his gay companion. Once more, then, he came back to camp. But time after time he left it again. His life in the wild made him stronger than ever.

One time Buck stayed away for weeks. And when he came back he was to find that the most terrible of all terrible things had happened. There was no camp to come back to. Roving Indians had attacked John Thornton and his partners. All three men were dead.

The bodies of the partners lay in camp for Buck to see. But where was his good, kindly master? Buck followed his footprints to a pool. He knew, then, in his heart, that the great love of his life lay at the bottom of it, dead.

All day Buck brooded by the pond, moved restlessly about the camp. There was a deep void in him. He could not eat nor drink. For hours — days — weeks — poor Buck guarded the pond and moaned.

There came the night of the full moon. Lying alone and weeping — yes, weeping beside the pool where John Thornton lay — Buck suddenly lifted his kingly head. He was hearing calls again — not only one, but many — coming from the forest. They seemed more compelling than ever. And, as never before, he was ready to obey.

Buck barked softly to say good-by to his dearest companion. Then, like a shadow in the moonlight, he took off to the forest. Standing in a clearing, he saw a pack of wolves. Not one wolf — a pack! Buck stood motionless at the sight of them — then he raised his head up high. He was sensing the same need he had felt when he had fought the hated Spitz for his place in the trace.

"I AM A LEADER AND A LEADER MUST LEAD!"

Buck looked at the wolfpack. They were all standing still — seemingly awed by his size and his air of regal command. Then, suddenly, one wolf

leaped forward to attack him. Like a flash, Buck struck, breaking his neck. Then three others tried to fight him. Buck made short work of them, too.

At last he had conquered. The wolf pack was his to command and obey. Those who were left came cautiously close. Buck stood on guard until he knew they had surrendered. Then he let them sniff noses with him in a half-savage, half-friendly fashion.

All began to yelp in a loud and lonely chorus. Buck starting yelping strangely, too. Then, turning, he dashed on through the forest. The wolf pack followed him obediently. It was as though they understood Buck's code:

"I AM A LEADER AND A LEADER MUST LEAD!"

Months later, roving Indians who had helped to kill John Thornton were savagely attacked by what they called a Ghost Dog. It happened in the valley where John Thornton's last camp had been made. So brutal was the attack that after it took place no Indian ever dared to enter that valley. They called it the place of the Evil Spirit.

But the valley was not such a place to Buck. It was his own and here he was king. He kept it an enchanted place in memory of his love for his master. He would return to the pool again and again — and sit there and mourn for John Thornton — mourn until he heard the strange call of the wild again —

His own wolf pack would follow him into this enchanted valley. He was their king, they would tell him, and he must lead them on. Then Buck would leap up — the tallest among them — a giant of a dog. He would run — and even the forest seemed to listen to his great throat chanting:

"I AM A LEADER AND A LEADER MUST LEAD!"

He was singing the song of his own young world. And wherever he ran, the wolf pack followed. That song, too, was the song of the pack. They knew Buck had answered the call of the wild.